J. Moore Neligan

Atlas of Cutaneous Diseases

Anatiposi

J. Moore Neligan

Atlas of Cutaneous Diseases

Reprint of the original.

1st Edition 2023 | ISBN: 978-3-38230-544-4

Anatiposi Verlag is an imprint of Outlook Verlagsgesellschaft mbH.

Verlag (Publisher): Outlook Verlag GmbH, Zeilweg 44, 60439 Frankfurt, Deutschland
Vertretungsberechtigt (Authorized to represent): E. Roepke, Zeilweg 44, 60439 Frankfurt, Deutschland
Druck (Print): Books on Demand GmbH, In de Tarpen 42, 22848 Norderstedt, Deutschland

ATLAS OF CUTANEOUS DISEASES.

ATLAS

CUTANEOUS DISEASES.

BY

J. MOORE NELIGAN, M. D. EDIN. M. R. I. A.

HONORARY DOCTOR OF MEDICINE, TRINITY COLLEGE, DUBLIN,
FELLOW OF THE KING AND QUEEN'S COLLEGE OF PHYSICIANS IN IRELAND,
HONORARY FELLOW OF THE COLLEGE OF PHYSICIANS OF SWEDEN,
HONORARY MEMBER OF THE CORK MEDICAL ASSOCIATION,
PHYSICIAN TO JERVIS-STREET HOSPITAL,
LECTURER ON THE PRACTICE OF MEDICINE IN THE DUBLIN SCHOOL OF MEDICINE,
ETC., ETC.

PHILADELPHIA:
BLANCHARD & LEA.
1859.

PREFACE.

My chief object in the publication of this book of Plates of Cutaneous Eruptions is to supply the student and junior practitioner with a work moderate in size and cheap in price, which can be readily referred to in the study of what is admittedly an obscure class of diseases. The difficulties in its preparation have been much greater than I at first anticipated; for I have endeavoured, as far as possible, to combine faithfulness in representation with accuracy of finish, without which it could not prove a faithful guide. To secure correctness in the design, the daguerreotype has been employed in several of the illustrations, in order to aid the artist in accurately reducing the figures, and retaining the exact proportions between the size of the eruption and the part of the body affected: for this purpose I have found the daguerreotype superior to photography, for while the former tends rather to heighten and fully develop the asperities of any given object, the latter softens them down, and often removes them altogether.

As regards the arrangement adopted, I have followed the classification proposed in my "Treatise on Diseases of the Skin;" and the letterpress given with the plates consists simply of a short description of each figure, with a reference for an account of the disease to the chapter and page of the book, in which it is fully described.* Nevertheless, although it thus becomes a supplement to that volume, it may be used with any other treatise on diseases of the skin.

* In reproducing the work these references have been altered to adapt them to the American Edition of the "Treatise," the two volumes thus forming together a complete system of Pathology and Treatment. — AM. PUBLISHERS.

(v)

My acknowledgments are due to Messrs. Forster and Co., by whom the plates were lithographed and printed in colours. To Mr. W. C. Forster of that firm I am especially indebted for the warm interest he took in the progress of the work, and the valuable assistance he afforded me, during the last three years while it was in preparation. It is also to his talented pencil I owe the drawings from which the lithographic illustrations were taken, except in the few cases where it is otherwise stated in the text.

For the liberality with which Messrs. Fannin and Co., the publishers, entered into my views in the bringing out of the work I must also express my obligations.

J. MOORE NELIGAN.

17, Merrion square East, Dublin,
June 11, 1855.

CONTENTS.

viii   CONTENTS.

PLATE I.

FIGURE 1. *Erythema simplex* (Chapter 2, page 31). This was the case of a man, aged 23, who was admitted into Jervis-street Hospital in 1852, in the last stage of Phthisis. The erythematous blush appeared, as depicted, a week before his death, and gradually faded away, no trace of it being left on the fifth day.

FIGURE 2. *Erythema læve* (Chapter 2, page 32). The red blush here appeared on the hip of a woman who had been confined for several weeks to bed with dropsical effusion into the extremities, depending on Bright's disease of the kidneys. It yielded to treatment without ulcerating, having completely disappeared within three weeks.

FIGURE 3. *Erythema papulatum* (Chapter 2, page 33). The eruption in this case appeared on the back of the hand of a gentleman, aged 36, who was at the time in excellent health. It faded away on the third day, no treatment having been used except the administration of some gentle saline purgatives.

FIGURE 4. *Erythema nodosum* (Chapter 2, page 33). This was the case of a boy, aged 9, admitted into Jervis-street Hospital in 1852. The eruption was at the time of three days' standing. He was dismissed cured within a fortnight.

FIGURE 5. *Erythema marginatum* (Chapter 2, page 32). This is an example of the variety of erythema which, from its seat, has been termed *palmaris*. When situated here, as in the case from which the illustration was taken, it is usually very obstinate, the irritation being kept up by constant friction, and by various matters with which the palm of the hand comes in contact. The man was a groom, an out-patient of Jervis-street Hospital, and had laboured under the disease for seven months.

FIGURE 6. *Erysipelas idiopathicum* (Chapter 2, page 38). The illustration is from a case under the care of my colleague Mr. James S. Hughes, in Jervis-street Hospital. The woman was aged 30, and this was the third attack she had ; it was produced each time by exposure to cold.

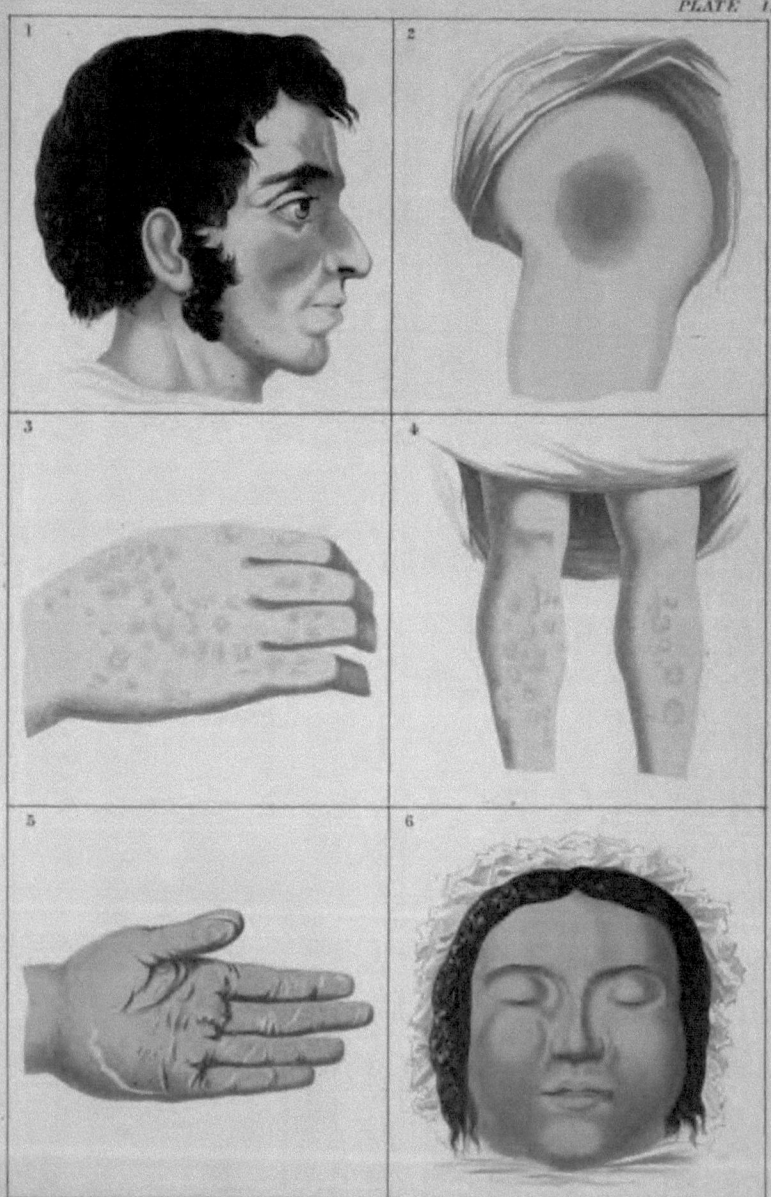

PLATE 1.

PLATE II.

FIGURE 1. *Urticaria febrilis* (Chapter 2, page 50). This was the case of a young man aged 17, who was under treatment in Jervis-street Hospital for an acute attack of pleurisy of the right side. On the fifth day, when the effusion was being rapidly absorbed and all symptoms of the fever were subsiding, he was attacked with shivering without any apparent cause, and on the following morning the nettle rash appeared, as here represented, on the front of the chest of the affected side.

FIGURE 2. *Urticaria conferta* (Chapter 2, page 51). The eruption is here represented on the fore-arm of a girl aged 18; it was confined to both fore-arms, where for months it obstinately resisted treatment, producing great suffering, especially at night. The origin of the rash could not be ascribed by the patient to any special cause.

FIGURE 3. *Urticaria evanida* (Chapter 2, page 51). The illustration of this form of nettle rash is taken from the case of a young girl, a dressmaker, an out-patient of Jervis-street Hospital. The eruption had existed for five years, with but little intermission, at the time she first came under my care.

FIGURE 4. *Urticaria tuberosa* (Chapter 2, page 52). In the case from which this drawing was taken the disease had been of 12 years duration. It was that of a lady aged about 45, who had spent many years of her life in India, where the rash first appeared. The sufferings she endured from it were extreme; it affected both legs equally and quite symmetrically.

FIGURE 5. *Roseola idiopathica*, var. *æstiva* (Chapter 2, page 57). An example of this disease in one of its most usual sites, occuring in a young lad aged 13 years.

FIGURE 6. *Roseola annulata* (Chapter 2, page 58). This drawing was taken from the case referred to in the above page of my Treatise on diseases of the Skin.

(15)

PLATE 2.

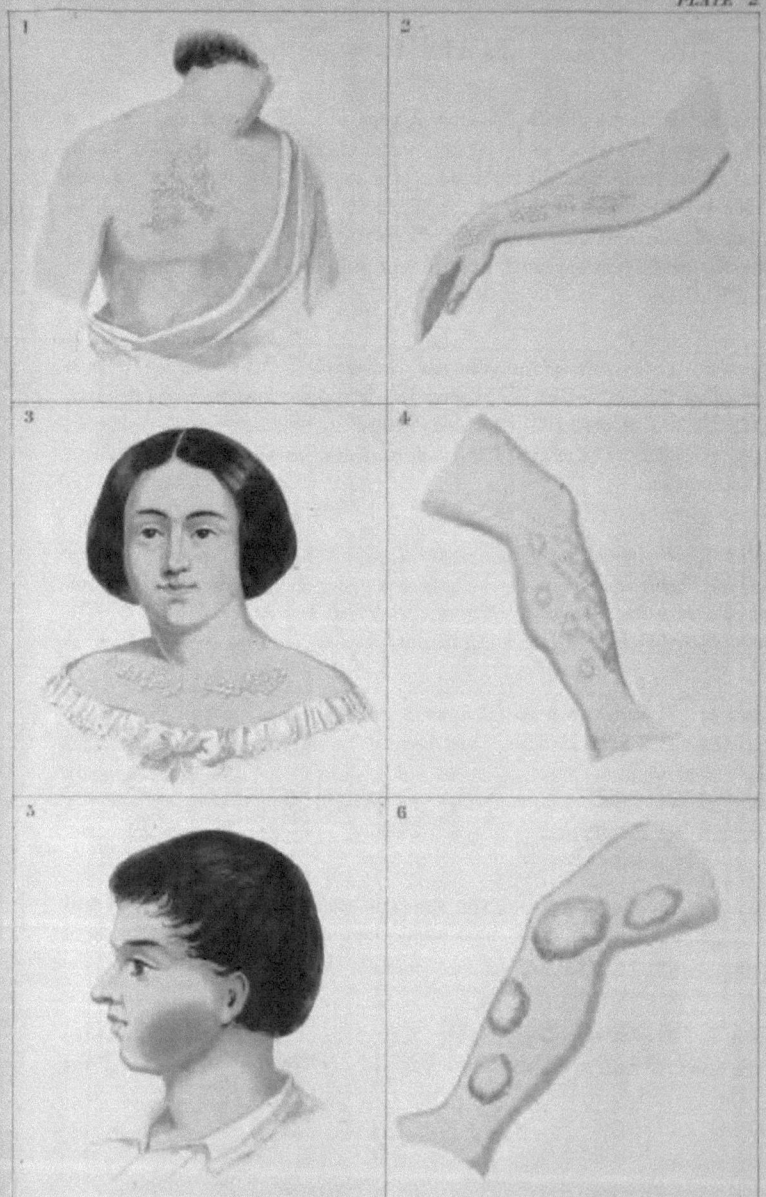

T. Sinclair's lith. Phila.

PLATE III.

FIGURE 1. *Eczema simplex* (Chapter 3, page 64). This is an example of the acute form of the disease appearing on the back of the right hand of a woman aged 56. She was of a full habit of body, a cook, and she ascribed its outbreak to the action of the fire. The drawing was made on the ninth day after the first appearance of the eruption.

FIGURE 2. *Eczema rubrum* (Chapter 3, page 65). The illustration in this case is from the legs of a woman aged 40, a patient in Jervis-street Hospital. The disease affected nearly every part of the body, and had been of several years duration. She was much reduced in health by the suffering she had gone through, but after three months stay in hospital she so far recovered as to be made an out-patient, and was ultimately completely cured, being now free from any return of the eruption for more than two years.

FIGURE 3. *Eczema impetiginodes* (Chapter 3, page 66). This drawing was taken from the left hand of the woman referred to in the description of Figure 1 of this plate. The eruption had appeared on it three weeks previously to its outbreak on the other hand; it eventually extended to every other part of the body, and proved very rebellious to treatment.

FIGURE 4. *Eczema chronicum* (Chapter 3, page 66.). This illustration is from the ear and side of the face of a child aged 5 years, who had for six months suffered from the disease, the eruption being confined to the face and scalp, and affecting the ears with especial severity.

FIGURE 5. *Eczema faciei* (Chapter 3, page 67). Eczema of the face in a child aged 2 years. The eruption had been of ten months standing at the time the drawing was taken.

FIGURE 6. *Eczema capitis* (Chapter 3, page 68). This was an example of the inflammatory form of eczema of the scalp. The drawing was made from a child aged 5 years, in whom the disease had been at the time of three months standing.

PLATE 3.

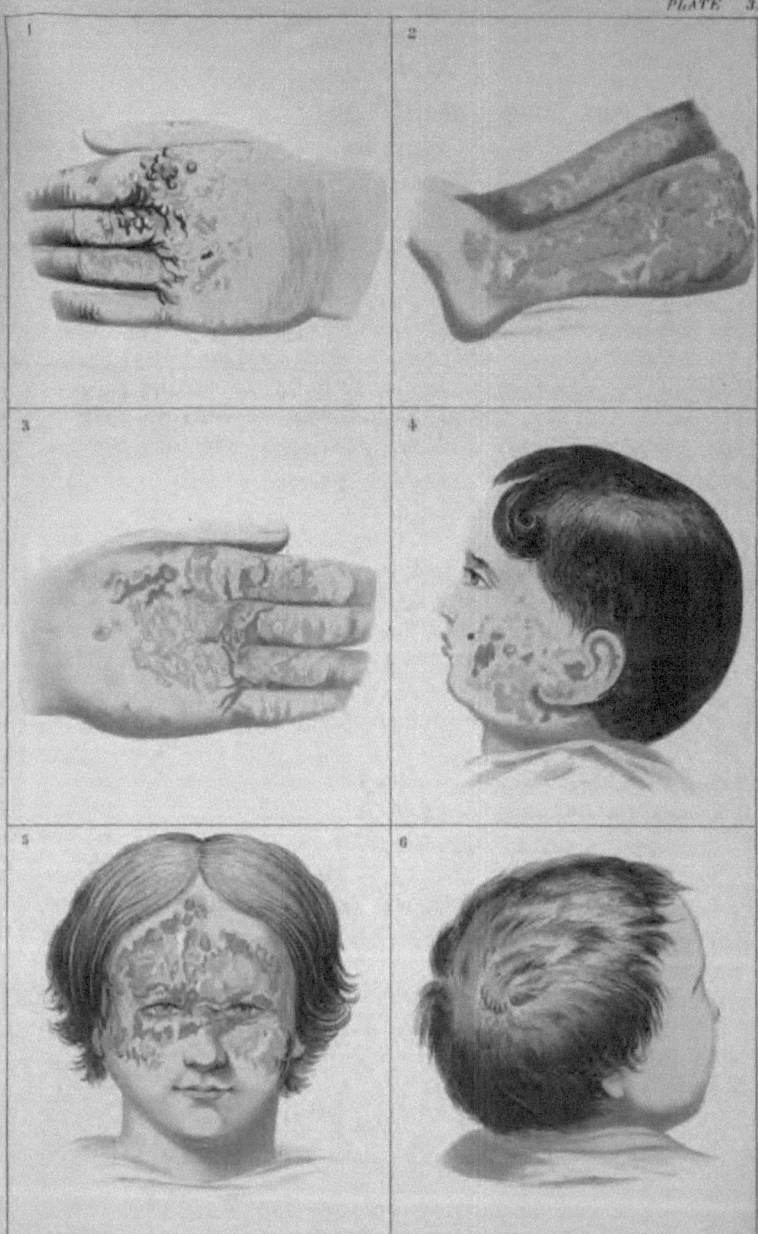

T. Sinclair's lith. Phila.

PLATE IV.

FIGURE 1. *Herpes phlyctenodes* (Chapter 3, page 78). A remarkably illustrative example of the disease, taken from the back of the neck of a girl aged 12. The eruption had been at the time of four days standing.

FIGURE 2. *Herpes zoster* (Chapter 3, page 81). The drawing represents this form of herpes appearing on its usual site; the eruption is shown on the fourth day after its appearance, when it extended from the sternum, passing beneath the mamma to the spine, some of the vesicles having attained their full magnitude and become opaque. It occurred on the right side of a boy aged 15.

FIGURE 3. *Herpes circinnatus* (Chapter 3, page 83). This was the case of a boy aged 9; there were three patches of the eruption on the neck, these two, the most characteristic, being situated as depicted just below the left ear and angle of the jaw. The disease had been of seven months standing at the time the drawing was made.

FIGURE 4. *Herpes iris* (Chapter 3, page 86). The case from which this drawing was made, presented the best defined example of this form of the eruption I have ever seen. The disease was situated on the anterior aspect of the most prominent portion of the shoulder of a child aged 6 years.

FIGURE 5. *Herpes squamosus* (Chapter 3, page 84). This illustration is reduced from the drawing in Cazenave's folio volume of plates. I have notes of three precisely analogous cases in my own practice, but as they occurred in persons in the higher walks of life, and all in one family, I was unable to procure drawings of any of them.

FIGURE 6. *Herpes capitis* (Chapter 3, page 84). The illustration here given of this form of herpes, about which so much difference of opinion exists, is from the scalp of a boy aged 5 years; there were two other patches, but not quite so large, on the side of the head; and one on the temple extending partly into the hairy scalp. This child's mother and a maid, both of whom applied the ointments and lotions ordered, became affected with herpes circinnatus on the backs of their hands; and his little sister was attacked with it on the scalp.

PLATE 4.

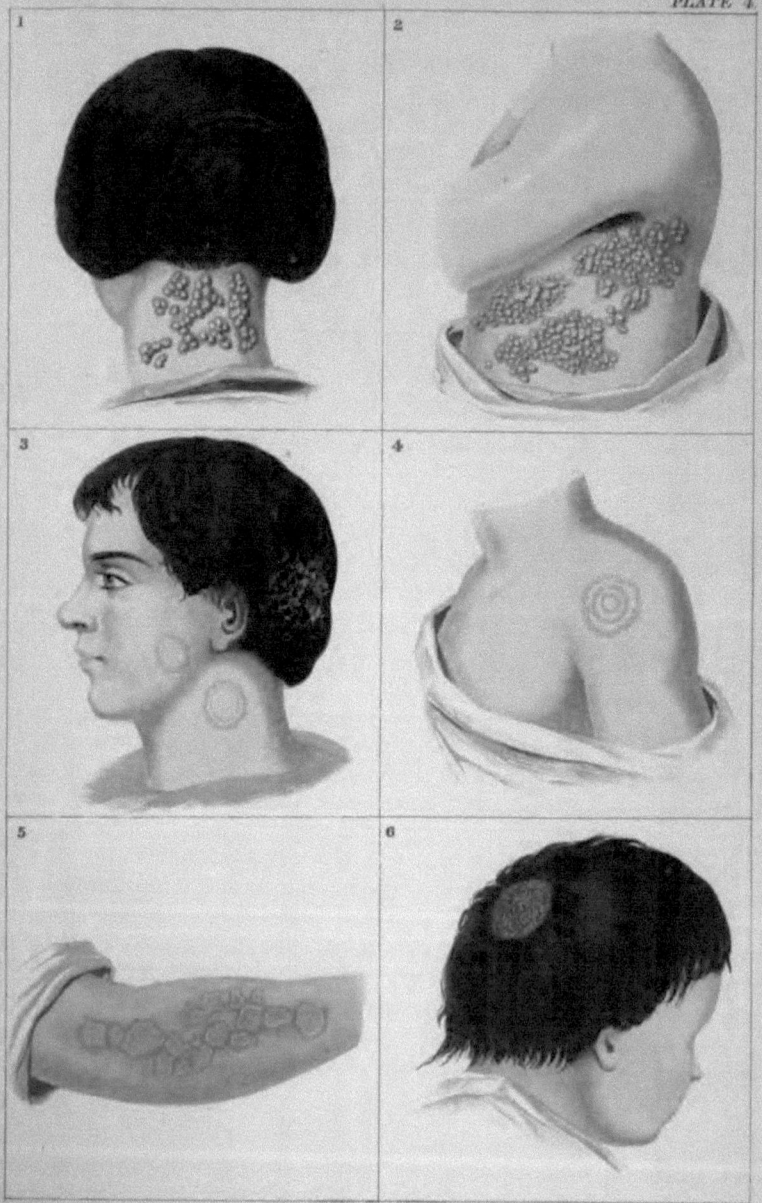

PLATE V.

FIGURE 1. *Pemphigus acutus* (Chapter 3, page 95). This is an accurate representation of a very acute and severe case of the disease occurring in a boy aged 8 years, of a well-marked scrofulous diathesis. The disease had lasted for several months at the time the drawing was taken, but had never lost its remarkably acute character, the duration being prolonged by the occurrence of continued outbreaks of the eruption, each being attended with well-marked febrile exacerbations. The fresh eruptions of the bullæ, as is seen on the extremities especially, usually took place in distinct rings surrounding the older patches of the disease. The sufferings in this case were so great, especially the loss of sleep caused by the violent itching, as to endanger the boy's life.

FIGURE 2. *Pemphigus chronicus* (Chapter 3, page 97). This is an example of the disease occurring in a young man aged 16. He had been for some time broken down in health, and the eruption of distinct large bullæ had continued to appear in successive crops, chiefly on the chest and upper extremities, for more than three months. It completely disappeared in the course of three weeks under the employment of nourishing diet and the internal use of iodide of iron, without any local applications.

FIGURE 3. *Pemphigus gangrænosus* (Chapter 3, page 97). For this graphic illustration the author is indebted to the kindness of Dr. George A. Kennedy, the drawing from which it is copied having been originally published in the Report of the Cork-street Fever Hospital for the years 1844–45. The case was that of a child aged 4 years. In some of the bullæ gangrenous action came on in about 48 hours after their appearance.

FIGURE 4. *Rupia simplex* (Chapter 3, page 103). In the case from which this drawing was taken the disease had been of three weeks' standing. It was that of a boy aged 9 years, of a scrofulous diathesis. He had previously suffered from a severe attack of scabies all over the body; and shortly after that eruption was cured by the ordinary local treatment, the characteristic bullæ of Rupia made their appearance on the back, followed by the greenish-brown crusts, as here depicted.

FIGURE 5. *Rupia prominens* (Chapter 3, page 103). This illustration was taken from a young man, aged 22, who had laboured under it for nearly five months at the time. He denied that he ever had any syphilitic affection, nor were any traces of that disease to be discovered on careful examination, such as cicatrized chancres, healed sore throat, nodes, &c.

PLATE 5.

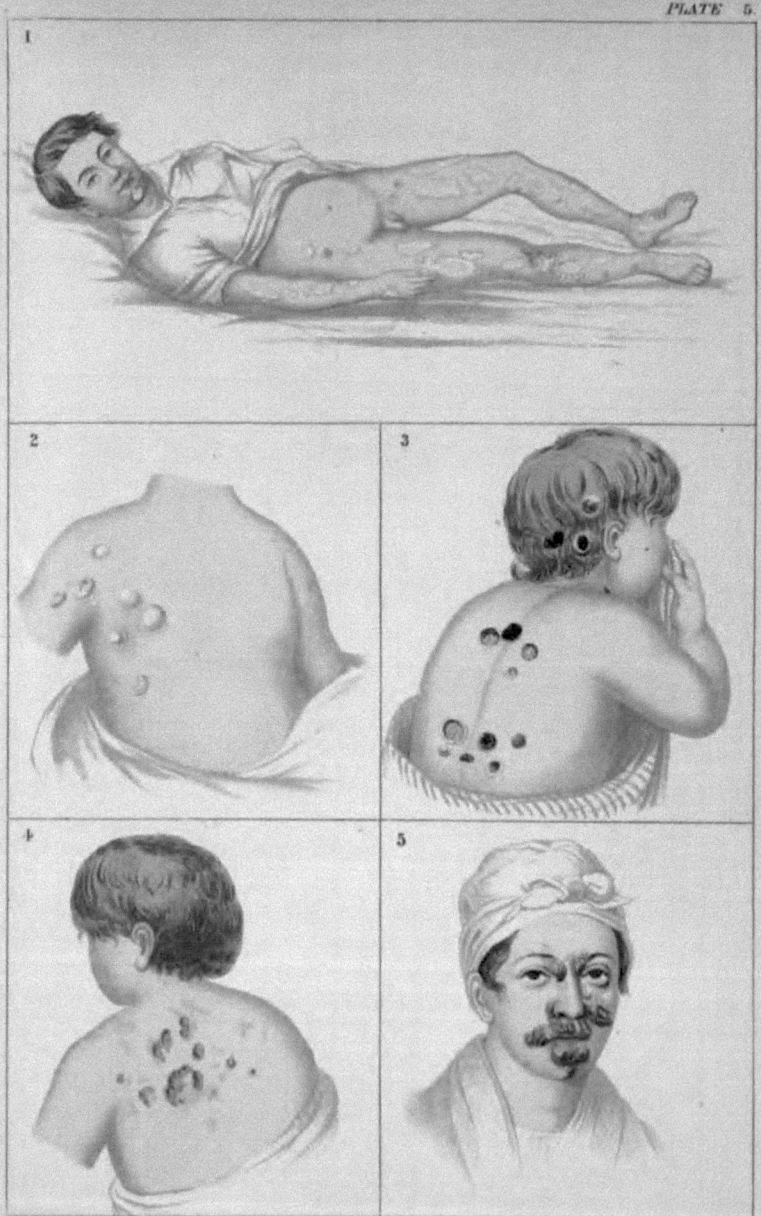

PLATE 6.

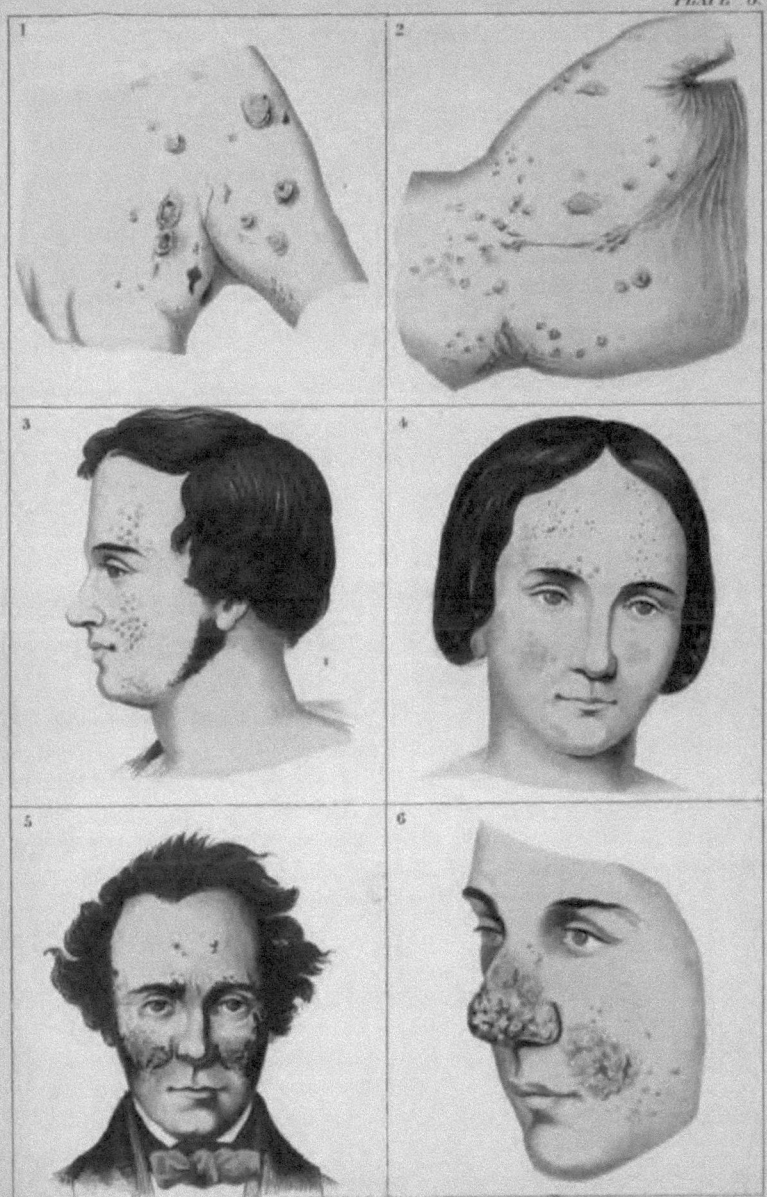

J. Crawley lith. Phil.

PLATE VI.

FIGURES 1 and 2. *Scabies* (Chapter 3, page 106). These two drawings are illustrative of the two stages which itch usually presents. They are from the hands of boys each aged between 10 and 11. In the first is seen the partly vesicular, partly purulent character of the eruption as it exists in the early stage, the disease in this example being of but three days standing; even thus early the *sillon* and *cuniculus* of the Acarus is visible. The second is an illustration of the purulent stage: the eruption here had existed for three weeks before the drawing was made. In Plate XVI. will be found representations of both the male and female Acarus scabiei.

FIGURE 3. *Acne simplex* (Chapter 4, page 118). This is an example of the most common form of acne in an aggravated condition, occurring on the face of a young man aged 24; the eruption was also present on his shoulders, neck and chest, there being at the same time several large, hardened pustules on the back.

FIGURE 4. *Acne punctata* (Chapter 4, page 119). The drawing in this case is from the face of a girl aged 18; she had suffered from outbreaks of the eruption in spring and autumn for the three previous years, the disease appearing chiefly on her forehead, her cheeks, and the back of her neck.

FIGURE 5. *Acne rosacea* (Chapter 4, page 120). This highly characteristic example of the eruption is after a daguerreotype by Professor Glukman and a drawing from life by Mr. Forster. The case was that of a man aged 45, who for many years had suffered from the disease, although he stated that he never indulged to excess in spirituous liquors, ascribing its occurrence to indigestion and dyspepsia from which he suffered much. Under treatment he improved so much as to be scarcely recognizable.

FIGURE 6. *Acne indurata* (Chapter 4, page 121). This illustration is from a drawing by Mr. Connolly of a patient in Jervis-street Hospital. He was a young man aged 18, a baker by trade, and had suffered from the disease for eighteen months; after three months treatment he was discharged cured, and there has been no return of the eruption, more than six years having since elapsed.

PLATE VII.

Figure 1. *Impetigo figurata* (Chapter 4, page 128). The illustration is from the face of a young man aged 20, admitted into Jervis-street Hospital on the eighth day of the eruption, when the disease was in its most inflammatory stage. It is after a daguerreotype by Professor Glukman and a drawing from life by Mr. Forster.

Figure 2. *Impetigo sparsa* (Chapter 4, page 130). Taken from the arm of a girl aged 11 years, also a patient in Jervis-street Hospital. The eruption had been of thirteen days standing at the time the drawing was made.

Figure 3. *Impetigo erysipelatodes* (Chapter 4, page 129). This drawing accurately represents the front of the abdomen of a woman aged 40, on the fifth day after the appearance of the characteristic pustules on the swollen and inflamed surface.

Figure 4. *Impetigo scabida* (Chapter 4, page 130). A highly characteristic example of this obstinate form of the eruption in a woman aged 28, an in-patient of Jervis-street Hospital. Both thighs were similarly affected, and scattered impetiginous pustules were also present over the hips, the front of the abdomen, and the legs, but the upper part of the body, the face and arms were quite free from any eruption. The disease had been of more than six months duration when she was admitted into hospital.

Figure 5. *Impetigo larvalis* (Chapter 4, page 131). The drawing in this case is from a child aged 3 years, in whom the eruption had existed for more than eighteen months. The scalp had been at first affected, but was at this time nearly well and the hair much grown.

Figure 6. *Impetigo capitis* (Chapter 4, page 131). From the back of the head of a boy aged 7 years, in whom the disease had been of three years duration. Both arms and the inside of the thighs were covered with an eruption of impetigo sparsa. The illustration is after a daguerreotype by Glukman.

PLATE 7.

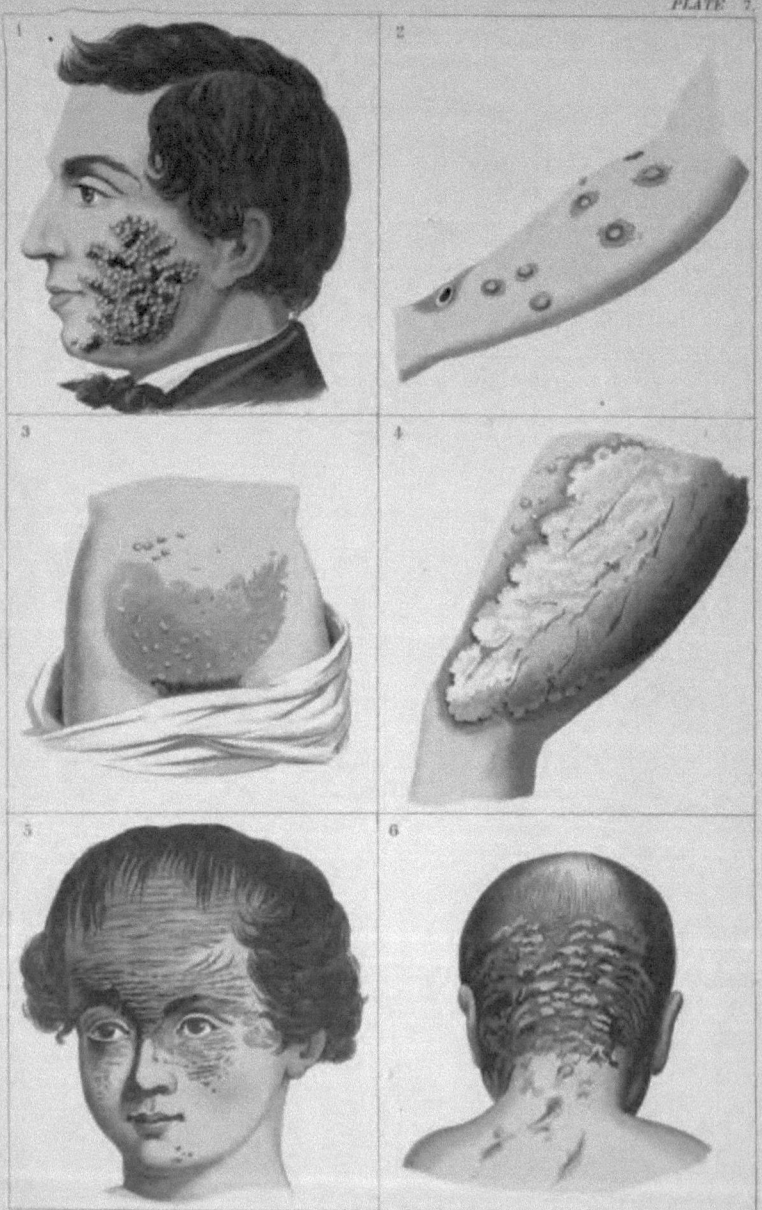

T. Sinclair's lith. Philad.

PLATE VIII.

FIGURE 1. *Ecthyma acutum* (Chapter 4, page 139). This drawing was taken from the leg of a young man aged 24, an in-patient of Jervis-street Hospital. He had been working as a labourer in railway excavations, exposed to much wet and cold, at the time the eruption first made its appearance. The disease had been of five weeks' duration at the time of his admission into hospital.

FIGURE 2. *Ecthyma chronicum* (Chapter 4, page 140). The eruption in this case is represented as it appeared on one of the legs of an unhealthy boy aged 7 years, of a well-marked scrofulous diathesis; he had been living in a low damp situation, ill-housed and ill-fed. The disease was present on the greater portion of the body, and was complicated with scabies and prurigo; it had existed for more than four months previous to his admission into Jervis-street Hospital.

FIGURE 3. *Lichen simplex* (Chapter 5, page 146). The disease as here represented existed on both arms of a large man of a full habit of body, aged 56. He was of very intemperate habits, and was liable to attacks of the eruption after every "hard bout" of drinking.

FIGURE 4. *Lichen circumscriptus* (Chapter 5, page 148). In this case the eruption was confined to the hands and fore-arms of a woman aged 30. It first appeared after she had been working in the open air for several days with her arms exposed to the heat of the sun, and had existed for three weeks at the time the drawing was made; the rash occurred with extraordinary symmetry on both arms.

FIGURE 5. *Lichen solitarius* (Chapter 5, page 148). This solitary patch was present on the back of a gentleman aged 30. It had existed there for three or four months previous to his coming under my care, and proved most rebellious to treatment.

FIGURE 6. *Lichen gyratus* (Chapter 5, page 148). Within the last eight months I have seen two cases of this very rare form of lichen. The one that is here represented occurred in a man aged 40, an out-patient of Jervis-street Hospital; previously to its appearance he had suffered for several months from attacks of acute pain resembling *Angina pectoris*. The other case was that of a gentleman aged 39, in whom it appeared on the back of the left shoulder, extending down the arm and spreading across towards the spine, exactly along the course of a very severe neuralgic attack from which he had suffered for several weeks. Both cases were very obstinate.

PLATE 6.

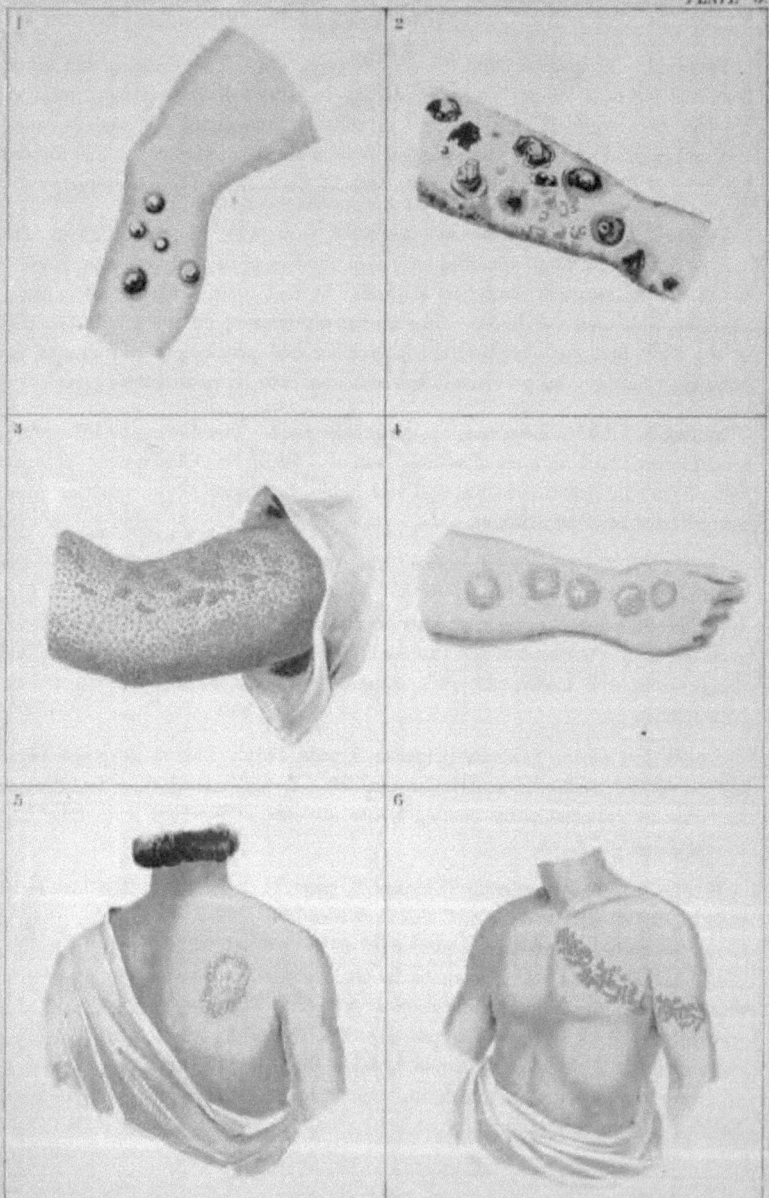

PLATE IX.

FIGURE 1. *Lichen strophulus intertinctus* (Chapter 5, page 149). A well-marked example of "Red Gum," appearing in an infant three weeks old; it was pretty generally diffused over the body.

FIGURE 2. *Lichen strophulus candidus* (Chapter 5, page 150). This illustration is taken from a twin sister of the infant delineated in Figure 1 of this plate. The rash appeared a few days later, and singularly enough assumed the form of "White Gum."

FIGURE 3. *Lichen agrius* (Chapter 5, page 150). The case from which this drawing was taken was that of a blacksmith aged 45, who had suffered under the disease in its most aggravated form for more than six years. He ascribed its origin to the great heat he was exposed to when working at his trade; it first commenced on the forehead, and gradually spread downwards to his nose and to the sides of the face. The covered parts of the body were quite free from it. He described the heat, pain, and itching as being most intolerable, rendering his life a burthen to him.

FIGURE 4. *Lichen agrius, dorsi manûs* (Chapter 5, page 151). An example of this severe eruption occurring in a cook aged about 40, who was an out-patient of Jervis-street Hospital. She had laboured under the disease for eight months at the time the drawing was made, and from the great suffering occasioned by the exposure of her hands to the heat of the fire had been compelled to relinquish her employment.

FIGURE 5. *Prurigo vulgaris* (Chapter 5, page 160). This illustration is from the arm of a boy aged 12; the disease had existed for three months, affecting the entire of the trunk and extremities, and was attended with the most intolerable itching.

FIGURE 6. *Prurigo senilis* (Chapter 5, page 162). The woman from whose arm this drawing was taken was the mother of the boy referred to in the last figure. They had both been inmates of the Poor-house, when the eruption first appeared. She was aged about 50, and in addition to the papular eruption, scabies and ecthyma were present at the same time on the extremities, rendering her case a most aggravated one; the body too was covered with pediculi.

PLATE 9.

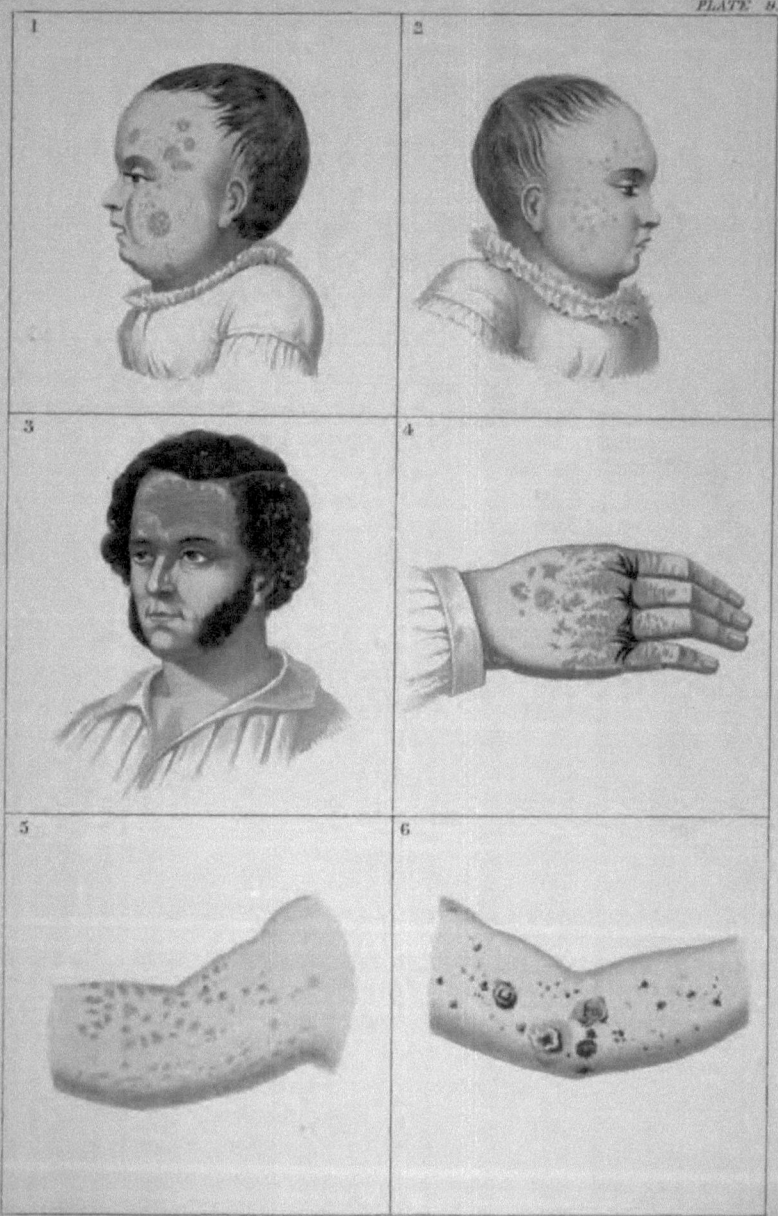

PLATE X.

FIGURE 1. *Psoriasis guttata* (Chapter 6, page 170). From the arm of a man aged 20. The disease had appeared three months previous to the drawing having been made: the eruption was generally and thickly distributed over the trunk and extremities.

FIGURE 2. *Psoriasis aggregata* (Chapter 6, page 172). The eruption in the case from which this drawing was made was on the arms, legs, and body of a woman aged 46, and had existed for nine or ten years, varying in intensity; at one time disappearing almost completely, and again recurring usually more severely than before. It was quite unattended with itching or constitutional irritation, all the bodily functions being well and healthily performed.

FIGURE 3. *Psoriasis inveterata* (Chapter 9, page 173). In this case the eruption, which was nearly altogether confined to the legs, had existed for twenty-six years. It was that of a gentleman aged 35, who had suffered from it from his youth. It caused much local irritation, compelling him to tear the affected surface, especially at night. That the constitution was also more or less engaged, was evidenced by the nails being brittle and having a diseased appearance, and the hair falling out, although there was no appearance of the eruption on the scalp.

FIGURE 4. *Psoriasis inveterata* (Chapter 6, page 173). This is an example of this form of the eruption, presenting the *tesselated pavement* appearance. The drawing is by Mr. Connolly, from a case under the care of Doctor Banks in the Whitworth Hospital.

FIGURE 5. *Psoriasis lepræformis* (Chapter 6, page 175). This illustration is after a daguerreotype by Glukman and a drawing from life by Mr. Forster, taken from the arm of a girl aged 11, a patient of Dr. Banks in the Whitworth Hospital.

FIGURE 6. *Psoriasis capitis* (Chapter 6, page 174). From the same case and by the same artists as Figure 5. It clearly establishes that lepra is but a form of Psoriasis.

PLATE 10

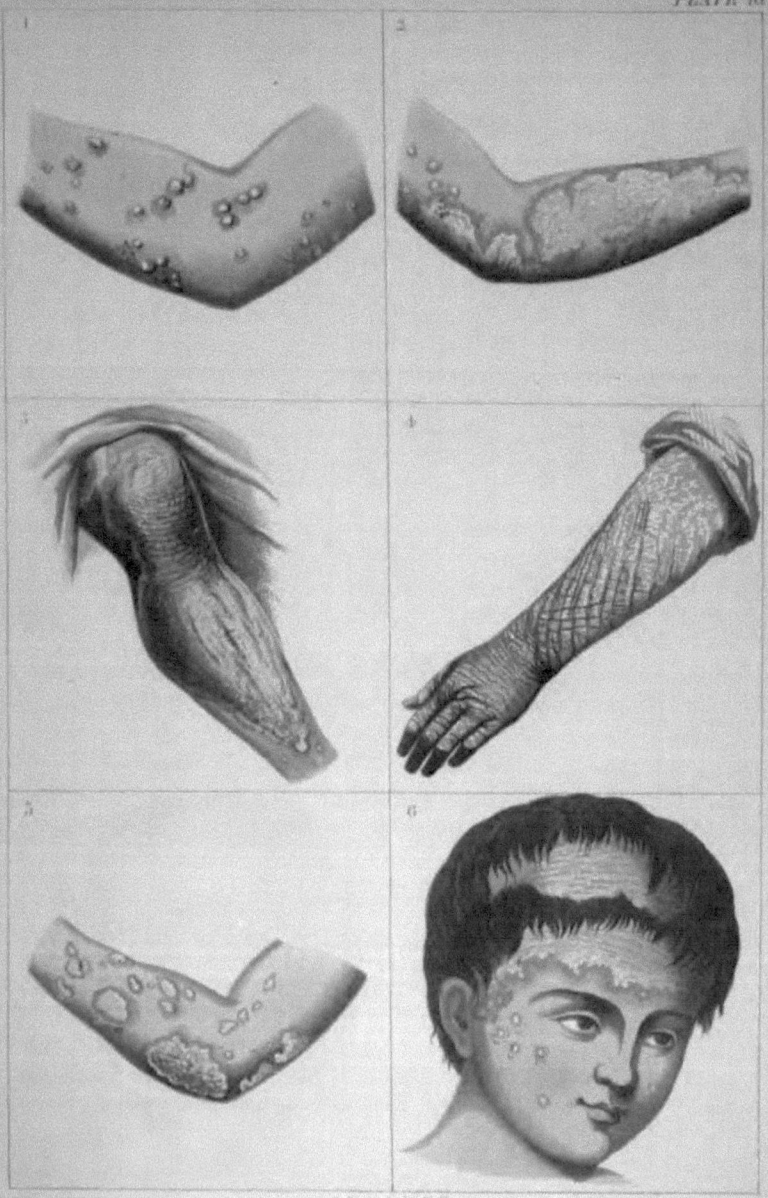

PLATE XI.

FIGURE 1. *Syphilitic Psoriasis*, var *lepræformis* (Chapter 12, page 292). This drawing was taken by Mr. Bragg from a man aged 35, who had been admitted into Jervis-street Hospital under the care of my colleague Mr. Ellis, for an injury of the head. He stated that the eruption, which was at this time confined to the legs, had been general over the body, and had first appeared more than six months previously, about five weeks after the primary sores had healed. Some of the scales, which could be readily detached, but were again reproduced within twenty-four hours, measured an inch in diameter.

FIGURE 2. *Pityriasis diffusa* (Chapter 6, page 191). The illustration here given is from the arm of a gentleman aged 20, formerly one of my pupils. The eruption was pretty generally diffused over the back, the chest, and the arms, varying in colour, being lightest in tint on the breast. It had been of several years duration, notwithstanding the continued use of numerous stimulating local applications, among others strong liquor potassæ, to which the patient had resorted. It yielded in some months to the arsenical treatment.

FIGURE 3. *Pityriasis capitis* (Chapter 6, page 193). In this case the boy, aged 13, was an out-patient of Jervis-street Hospital. At the time the drawing was made the disease had been of six years duration, having obstinately resisted the most varied plans of treatment employed by different medical men.

FIGURE 4. *Ichthyosis* (Chapter 7, page 200). This illustration is from a boy aged 15, who had been admitted into the Meath Hospital under the care of Dr. Lees. The disease was congenital as far as we could ascertain, and existed on nearly every part of the body, being especially developed on the most prominent surfaces; a patch such as is here represented was present on both sides of the face, and on both ears.

FIGURE 5. *Molluscum acutum* (Chapter 7, page 209). An example of this rare affection in a girl aged 16, for an opportunity of seeing which I am indebted to Dr. W. D. Moore. It was at the time of four months duration, and its origin could not be traced by the patient to contagion. The small tumours were scattered over both sides of the neck, the front of the chest, and through the hair. The artist had in this illustration the aid of a daguerreotype by Glukman.

FIGURE 6. *Molluscum chronicum* (Chapter 7, page 210). The illustration is after a drawing by Mr. Cooney, made for Dr. George A. Kennedy, to whom I am indebted for permission to use it. It was the case of a woman aged 40, and at the time the drawing was made the disease had been of several years' duration; of the ultimate result I know nothing.

(30)

PLATE II

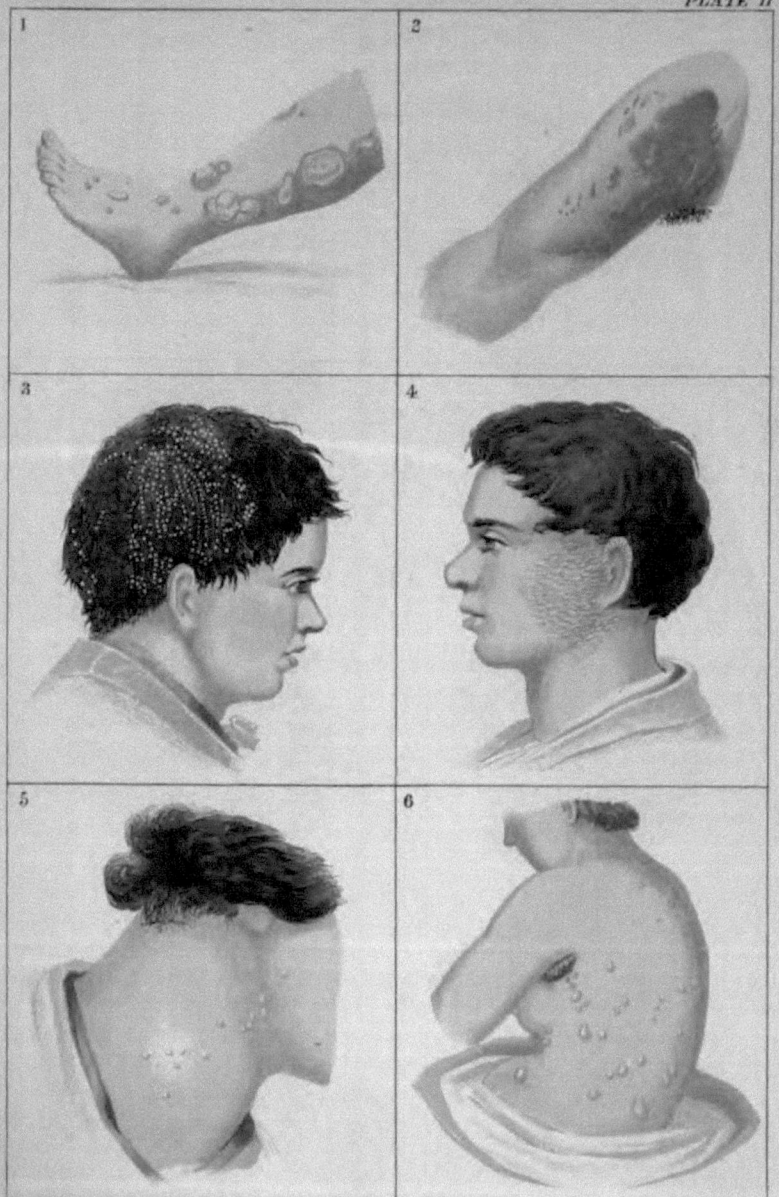

T. Sinclair's lith. Phila

PLATE XII.

FIGURE 1. *Stearrhœa flavescens* (Chapter 7, page 213). This is an example of that form of the disease originally described by Biett under the name of *Acne sebacea*. It occurred in a country girl aged 22, who was an in-patient of Jervis-street Hospital; and although it had been of three years' duration, was confined to the nose, as is here represented.

FIGURE 2. *Stearrhœo flavescens* (Chapter 7, page 213). An illustration of the more usual form of the disease, after a daguerreotype by Glukman and a drawing from life by Mr. Forster. The case was that of an unmarried female aged 35 years, and the disease she stated had existed on her face since she was twelve years old. It was completely removed after eight months' treatment.

FIGURE 3. *Stearrhœa nigricans* (Chapter 7, page 214). I have published a full account of the case from which this illustration is taken in the 19th Volume of the Dublin Quarterly Journal, where I have also stated at length my views as to the nature and pathology of the disease.

FIGURE 4. *Elephantiasis Grœcorum* (Chapter 7, page 217). The illustration of this disease is copied from Cazenave's Folio Plates of Diseases of the Skin, at present in course of publication.

FIGURE 5. *Spedalskhed* (Chapter 7, page 218). This drawing, illustrative of the Norwegian elephantiasis, is copied from the magnificent work of Danielssen and Boeck, in which the following description of the case is given : — A young woman aged 28, in whom the tubercles have become confluent and are covered with thick greyish-brown crusts, which sometimes reach the height of two inches. These crusts being removed, the tubercles present an ulcerated appearance. Both on the surface and in the interior of the tubercles reside millions of *acarides*, which we believe to be identical with *acarus scabiei*. The crusts are almost wholly composed of the dead bodies of these animalcules. The detached tubercles, which are not covered with crusts, as well as the still sound skin, have a dirty greyish colour.

FIGURE 6. *Elephantiasis Arabum* (Chapter 7, page 218). The drawing in this instance is from the leg of a woman aged 40, an out-patient of Jervis-street Hospital. The disease had been of seven years' standing, and only affected the left leg.

PLATE 12.

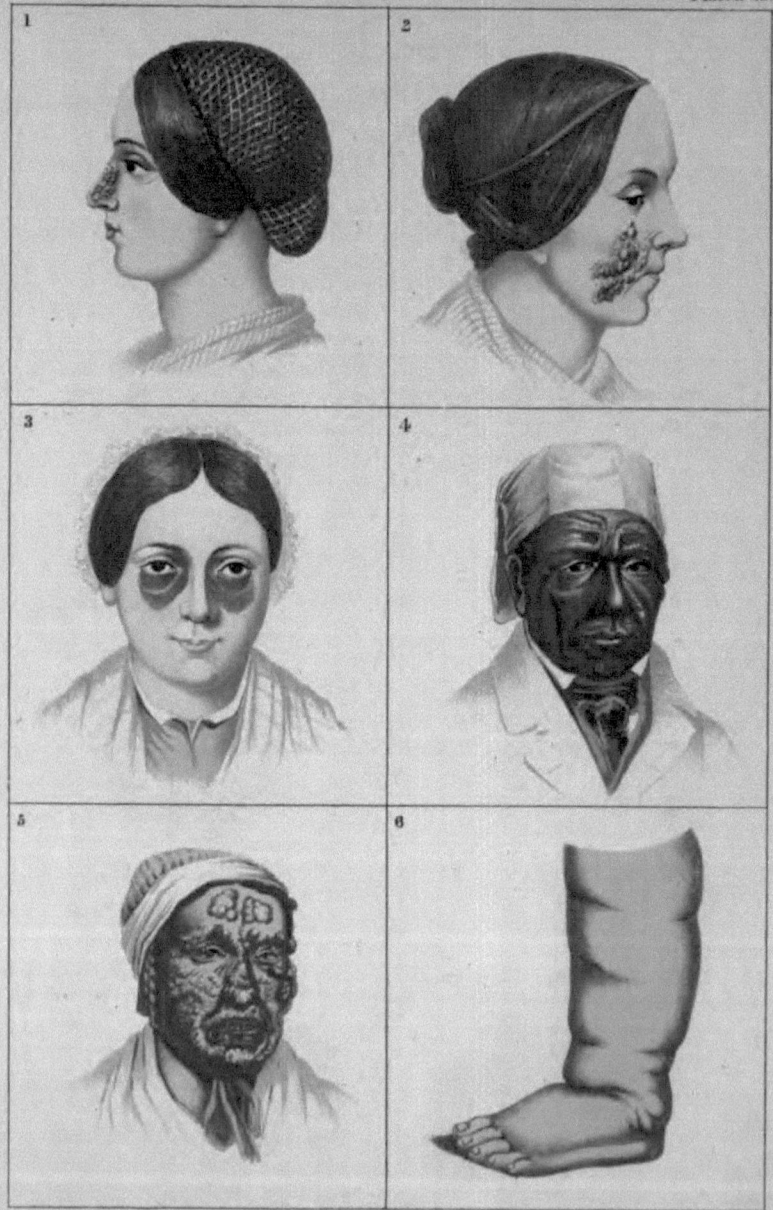

PLATE XIII.

FIGURE 1. *Purpura simplex* (Chapter 8, page 227). The drawing from which this illustration is copied, was taken from a man aged 30, an in-patient of Jervis-street Hospital. The disease had been at the time of five days standing, and was as thickly set over the rest of the body as is here exhibited on the shoulder. He left hospital well in less than three weeks, during which time there had not been any hemorrhage from the mucous surfaces.

FIGURE 2. *Purpura urticans* (Chapter 8, page 228). The disease in the case from which this illustration was taken, appeared on both lower extremities of a man aged 40, who had been much broken down from chronic disease and general debility, caused by want of food and other privations.

FIGURE 3. *Purpura hemorrhagica* (Chapter 8, page 229). I have thought it well to give a full-length drawing of this case, as it represents so admirably the general character of the disease. It is that of a child, at the time aged 6 years, and was originally published by me in the 28th Volume of the First Series of the Dublin Journal of Medical Science, as illustrative of the efficacy of large doses of oil of turpentine in this disease,— a plan of treatment since then put forward as original by others. This girl has been on three occasions in Jervis-street Hospital under my care with attacks of Purpura hemorrhagica, an interval of more than eighteen months elapsing between each, but none of her family, brothers or sisters, of whom there are several, father or mother, have had it. The drawing is by the late Mr. Neilan.

FIGURE 4. *Vitiligo* (Chapter 9, page 238). This illustration is from the side of a man aged 50, who was for several years affected with the discoloration on his chest, back, and sides.

FIGURE 5. *Albinoismus* (Chapter 9, page 237). The portrait of a girl aged 18. Her father and mother are fair but with the usual amount of colour; and of eight children, she and her sister, the two eldest, are alone affected. The sister, who is older, although an albino, is not so perfect an example as this girl.

PLATE 13.

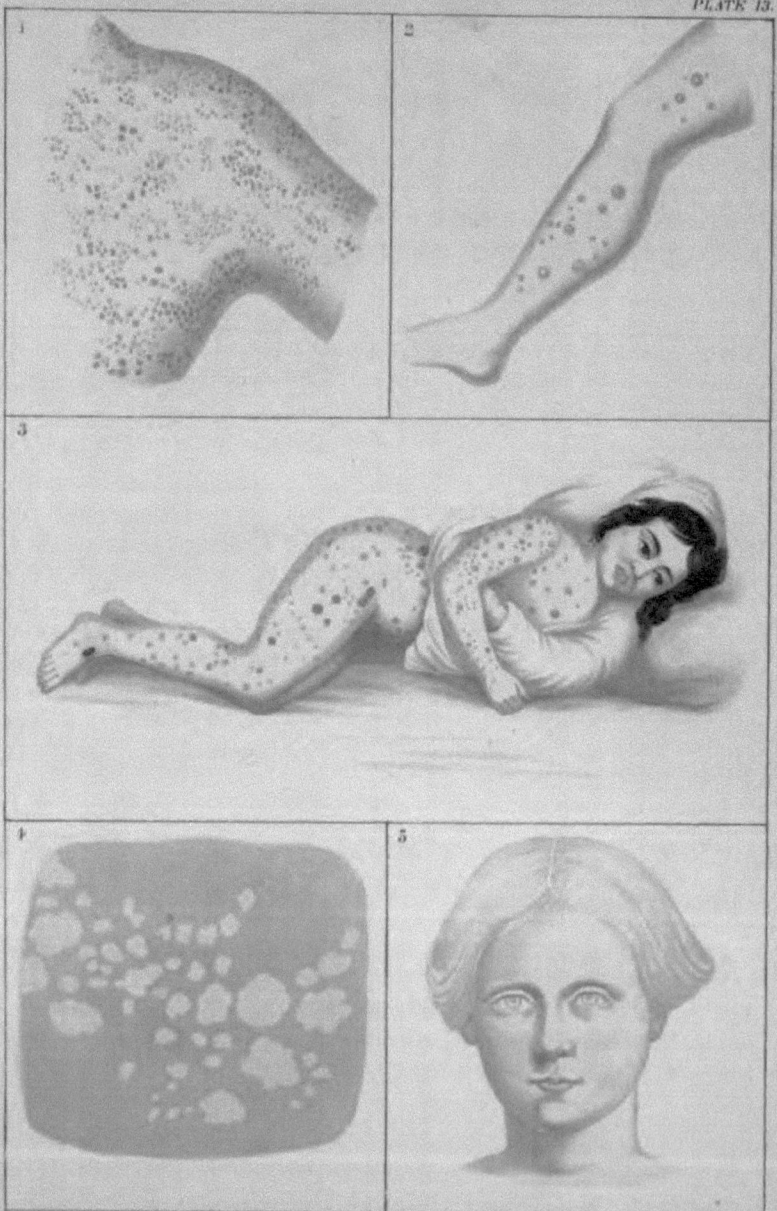

PLATE XIV.

FIGURE 1. *Nævus* (Chapter 7, page 224). In consequence of the singularity of the congenital marking of the skin in this case, and the curious history attached to it, I have been induced to give an illustration of it here. The boy, who is now aged 7 years, is covered, as is represented, along the neck and back with long silky hair, that along the spinous processes of the vertebræ being arranged somewhat like the mane of a horse. The skin beneath is of a reddish brown colour, and there are numerous other similar spots scattered over the body and extremities. The boy's mother is the wife of a coachman, and when about six months pregnant of this child she states that the stables having taken fire during the night, she went to the assistance of her husband, who was endeavouring to get the horses out. In the midst of the smoke she had to hold one of the horses around the neck for some time, and try to restrain his violence. This alarmed her very much at the time, but she soon thought no more of the occurrence until her child was born thus marked. For an opportunity of seeing the case I am indebted to Dr. Lees. The drawing is by Mr. Bragg.

FIGURE 2. *Lupus superficialis* (Chapter 10, page 247). This illustration is from a woman aged 45, an out-patient of Jervis-street Hospital. The disease had been of thirteen years standing, during which time it was gradually spreading across the nose, leaving its white cicatrix behind.

FIGURE 3. *Lupus serpiginosus* (Chapter 10, page 248). For the drawing in this case I am indebted to Staff-surgeon Mandeville. It was taken from a soldier of the 66th Regiment under his care, and is highly characteristic of this form of the disease when confined to the face.

FIGURE 4. *Lupus devorans* (Chapter 10, page 250). The case of a woman aged 28, a patient of Jervis-street Hospital. The disease had been of eighteen years duration at the time of her admission, and after five months treatment in the hospital the surface had healed over, and the progress of the ulceration was quite arrested. The illustration is after a daguerreotype by Geary, Brothers, and a drawing from life by Mr. Forster.

FIGURE 5. *Lupus devorans* (Chapter 10, page 252). This characteristic representation of "Jacob's ulcer" is after a daguerreotype by Glukman and a drawing from life by Mr. Forster. The woman, who was aged 35, had suffered under this frightful affection for eighteen years. She had been originally in my wards in Jervis-street Hospital, and was afterwards in the Hospital for Incurables, under the care of Professor Geogheghan; the right eye was at this time completely destroyed, and the ulceration was extending slowly but surely to the left.

PLATE XV.

Figure 1. *Sycosis* (Chapter 11, page 274). The portrait is that of a man aged 40, who had laboured under this obstinate affection for many years without obtaining any permanent relief, the eruption at times healing up on some of the patches but to break out again on others. Ultimately the hair-bulbs were quite destroyed in parts, and several *bald* patches left on the chin, these with the hardened elevations and attendant pustules produced very great disfigurement in addition to the pain and suffering occasioned. After several months treatment in Jervis-street Hospital and also as an out-patient, all traces of the eruption disappeared. It is one of the cases in which the plan of treatment recommended in my Treatise on Diseases of the Skin was found successful. The illustration is after a daguerreotype by Glukman.

Figures 2 and 3. *Porrigo* (Chapter 11, page 265). These figures represent the aspect of the eruption as situated on the scalp and on the body. Figure 2 is after a drawing by Mr. Connolly, from a girl aged 12, who had been afflicted with the disease for six years; it was the most aggravated example of the affection which has occurred in my practice, and yet was perfectly cured by the mild and simple plan of treatment I have ventured to recommend. At the time the girl—Mary Brown—was admitted into Jervis-street Hospital in the year 1846, the hair bulbs were completely destroyed, and consequently when she was re-admitted in 1852, labouring under scrofulous enlargement of the glands of the neck, the head was completely bald, although there had not been the least return of the disease for the intervening six years. I have records, however, of many cases in which the hair-bulbs not having been destroyed, the hair grew freely after recovery. Figure 3 is after a drawing by the late Mr. Neilan, from a child aged 4 years; it is an example of the extent to which, at times, though very rarely, porrigo appears on the body.

PLATE 15

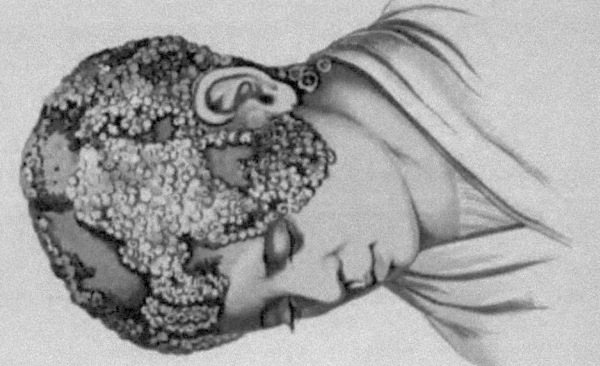

T. Sinclair's Lith. Philada.

PLATE XVI.

FIGURE 1. *Acarus scabiei* (Chapter 3, page 108). The *female* itch insect magnified 120 diameters, after Bourguignon. The abdominal aspect is here shown.

FIGURE 2. *Acarus scabiei* (Chapter 3, page 109). The *male* itch insect magnified 200 diameters, after Bourguignon. The abdominal aspect is also shown in this instance.

FIGURE 3. *Steatozoon folliculorum* (Chapter 4, page 119). Two varieties of this insect are here represented after Gustav Simon; they are both magnified 300 diameters. The one is long, slender, with three pairs of legs; the other short with a rounded body and four pairs of legs.

FIGURE 4. *Microsporon mentagrophytes* (Chapter 11, page 276). The drawings from which this lithograph is taken were kindly made for me by Dr. Steele, being the result of a microscopic examination by him of a hair taken from the chin of a gentleman affected with true Sycosis, who was under my care. Dr. Carte also examined the same specimen. Fig. A represents a portion of the hair-sheath separated from the hair; *a* the outer membrane of the sheath; *b* the contents, containing granular matter, and *d* groups of roundish oval bodies; *c* portion of the membrane torn, leaving a fimbriated extremity; the latter was observed to be the case in a specimen of a healthy hair-sheath which was also torn. Fig. B represents some of the contents of the hair-sheath floating in the water employed in mounting the specimens. Both were drawn with a camera, and magnified 400 diameters.

FIGURE 5. *Achorion Schonleinii* (Chapter 11, page 268). Portion of the matter which forms the external layer of Porrigo magnified 500 diameters. The filaments of the fungus are well shown; they are much branched, not jointed, and some of them contain in their interior very fine granulations, which represent the mycelium of the vegetable parasite.

FIGURE 6 is copied from Robin (*Histoire Naturelle des Végétaux Parasites*, Paris, 1853). It represents a portion of epidermic crust taken from the scalp in a case of Porrigo, magnified 580 diameters. *a* is the epidermic orifice of a sebaceous gland or hair follicle; *b, c, d, e, f,* are groups of spores adherent to the epidermic scales. It will be seen that the latter bear a close resemblance to those found by Dr. Steele in the fungus of Sycosis.